My 1st Classic Story

How the
Camel
Got Its
Hump

a retelling by Christianne C. Jones

illustrated by Ronnie Rooney

PICTURE WINDOW BOOKS
a capstone imprint

My First Classic Story is published by Picture Window Books
A Capstone Imprint
151 Good Counsel Drive, P.O. Box 669
Mankato, Minnesota 56002
www.capstonepub.com

Originally published by Picture Window Books, 2005.

Library of Congress Cataloging-in-Publication Data
Jones, Christianne C.
How the camel got its hump / retold by Christianne C. Jones ;
illustrated by Ronnie Rooney.
p. cm. — (My first classic story)
Adaptation of a story by Rudyard Kipling,
originally published in his Just so stories.
Summary: When hard-working animals complain to
"the magic desert watcher" about camel's laziness, the
watcher agrees to make things more fair.
ISBN 978-1-4048-6075-9 (library binding)
ISBN 978-1-4048-7358-2 (paperback)
[1. Camels—Fiction. 2. Laziness—Fiction. 3. Magic—Fiction.
4. Deserts—Fiction.] I. Rooney, Ronnie, ill. II. Kipling, Rudyard,
1865-1936. Just so stories. III. Title.
PZ7.J6823Ho 2011
[E]—dc22   2010003631

Art Director: Kay Fraser
Graphic Designer: Emily Harris

Printed in the United States of America in Stevens Point, Wisconsin.
062011   006273

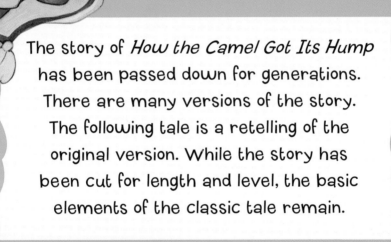

The story of *How the Camel Got Its Hump* has been passed down for generations. There are many versions of the story. The following tale is a retelling of the original version. While the story has been cut for length and level, the basic elements of the classic tale remain.

It was another hot day in the desert.
Horse, Dog, and Ox worked and worked.

While they worked, Camel just stood
around. All he ever said was "Humph!"

On Monday, Horse talked to Camel.
"Camel, come run with us."

"Humph!" said Camel.

On Tuesday, Dog talked to Camel.
"Camel, come fetch with us."

"Humph!" said Camel.

On Wednesday, Ox talked to Camel.
"Camel, come plow with us."

"Humph!" said Camel.

On Thursday, Horse, Dog, and Ox told their owner about Camel.

"I'm sorry. There's nothing I can do. You three will just have to work harder," said their owner.

On Friday, Horse, Dog, and Ox called a meeting.

They met with the magic desert watcher.

"Camel won't work. We do everything.
It's not fair!" they cried.

"It isn't fair," he said. "I will take care of it."

On Saturday, the magic desert watcher found Camel. "Camel, I hear you won't do any work."

"Humph!" said Camel.

"I knew you would say that. I wouldn't say it again, if I were you. You never know what could happen," said the magic desert watcher.

"Humph!" said Camel.

"That does it!" yelled the magic desert watcher. He twirled, yelled, and placed a spell on Camel.

A large hump slowly started to grow on Camel's back.

"What's going on?" asked Camel.

"You have brought that hump upon yourself," said the magic desert watcher. "Now you are going to work."

"How can I work with this giant hump?"
asked Camel.

"Your hump will help you work. It stores food and water. Now you can work without stopping," said the magic desert watcher.

On Sunday, Camel joined Horse, Dog, and Ox in the desert.

None of the animals said a word about
Camel's hump.

Camel still doesn't behave, but he now does his share of the work.

And that's how the camel got its hump.

The End